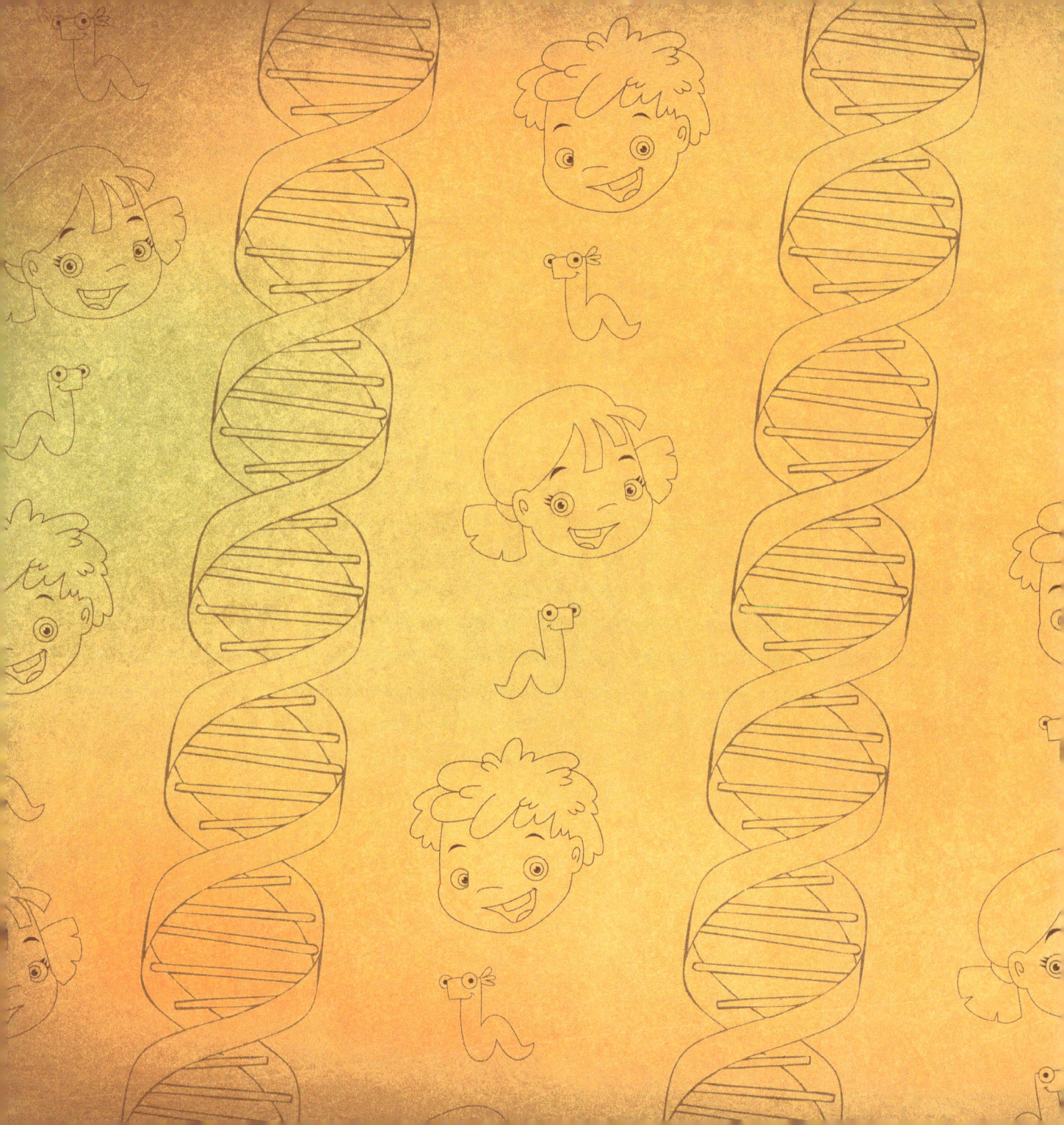

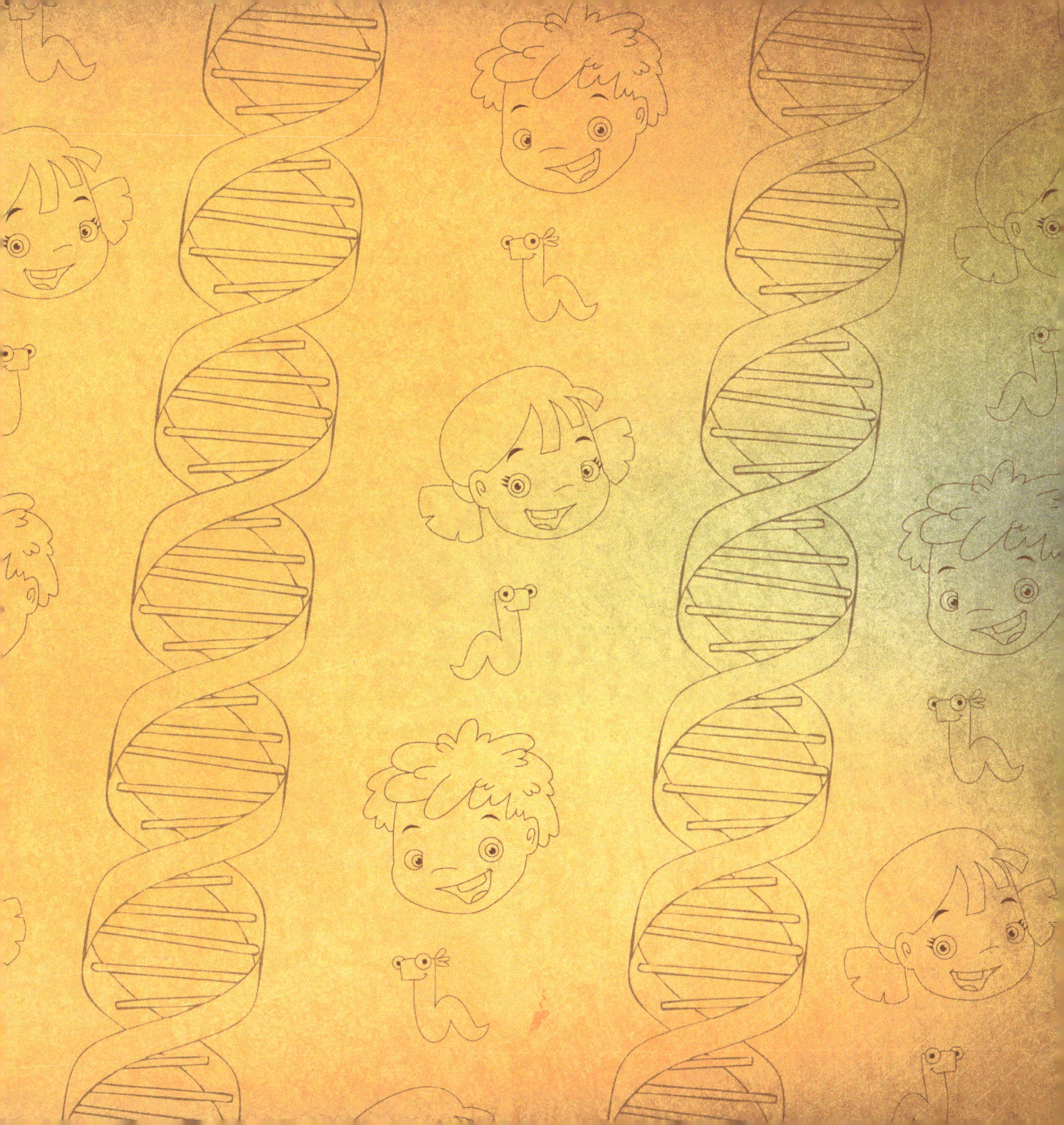

Illustrated by Marcin Poludniak
Written by Jennifer Gaither

Copyright © 2022 by Puppy Dogs & Ice Cream, Inc.
All rights reserved. Published in the United States
by Puppy Dogs & Ice Cream, Inc.

ISBN: 978-1-957922-11-9
Edition: September 2022

PDIC and Puppy Dogs & Ice Cream are trademarks of
Puppy Dogs & Ice Cream, Inc.

For all inquiries, please contact us at:
info@puppysmiles.org

To see more of our books, visit us at:
www.PuppyDogsAndIceCream.com

This book is given with love

To _____

From _____

We often think
that our thoughts are unique,
But if all our thoughts
could stand up and speak...

Through thousands of years of Earth's history...
No two people are the same, and **they never will be.**

Each person's special a unique combination...
Of shape, color, and size, **a perfect compilation!**

The way you look is special
there's only one of you...
You're completely original
and should celebrate that too!

It's great to feel good
about the body you embrace...
**Your own special character
and your own special face!**

Now, I'm not saying
you won't notice or compare...
You will see differences,
don't ignore that they're there.

You can still appreciate
everything that is you...
**And recognize everyone's
own specialness too!**

Don't judge other people for their shape or their size...

Look at your life
through compassionate eyes.

You can use this principle
on yourself the same way...

Don't be harsh on yourself,
and be kind every day.

Inside and out,
we're all interesting creatures...

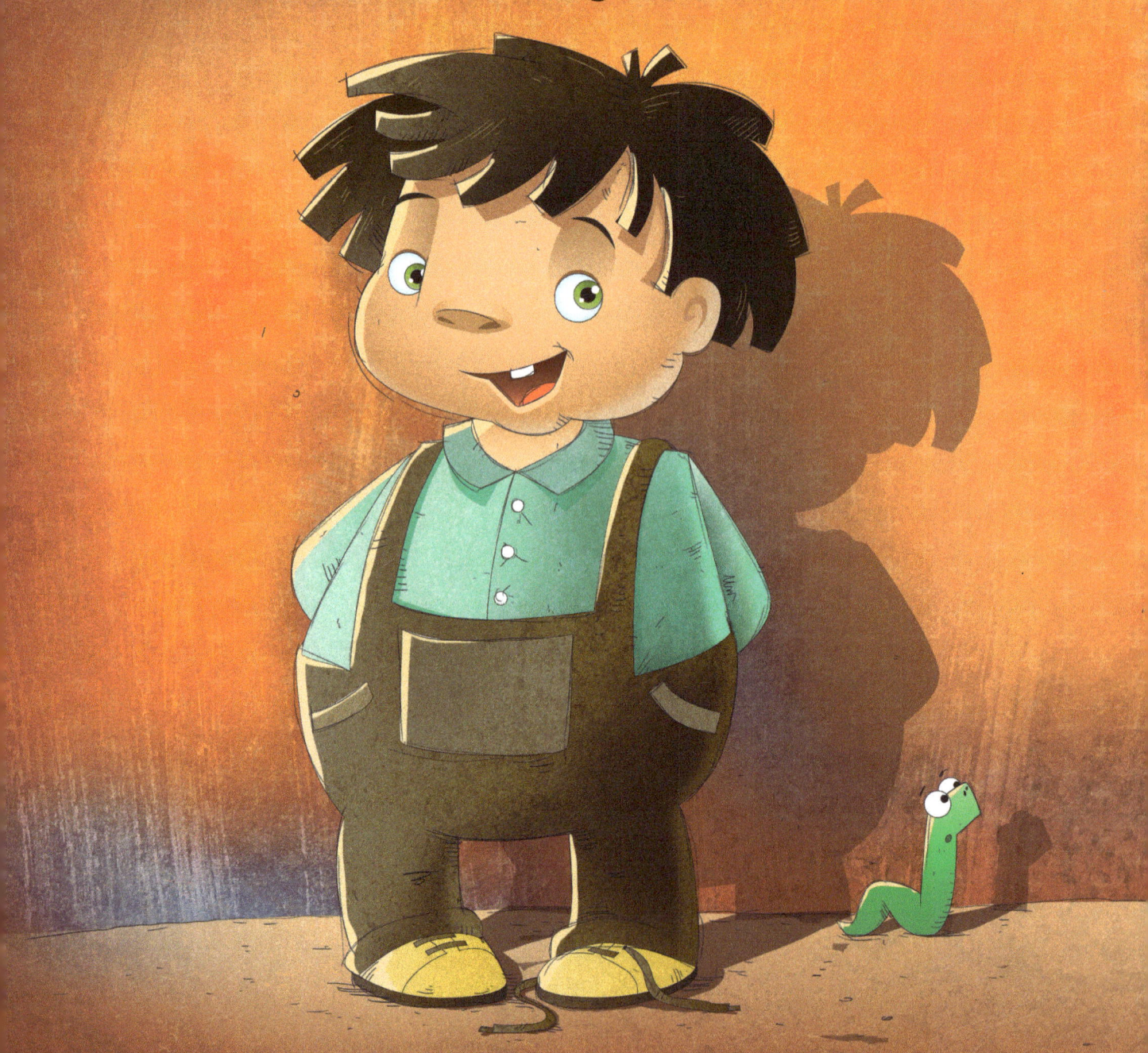

With our different mix
of familial features.

A belly that is round,
or teeth that are small...

Freckles all over,
or being short or tall.

Especially if you're not typical or textbook.

But it's silly to feel stressed, it's nothing you can control...

So accept your appearance, that should be your goal.

If we all looked the same,
how boring it would be...
We couldn't tell the difference
between you and me!

But it's part of the plan
that we differ from each other...
**It's our differences that help
bring joy to one another.**

Shift your thinking now,
on how to be...
Your very best self,
not comparing he or she.

Instead, try to compare
in a different way...
Tracking your own changes
since yesterday.

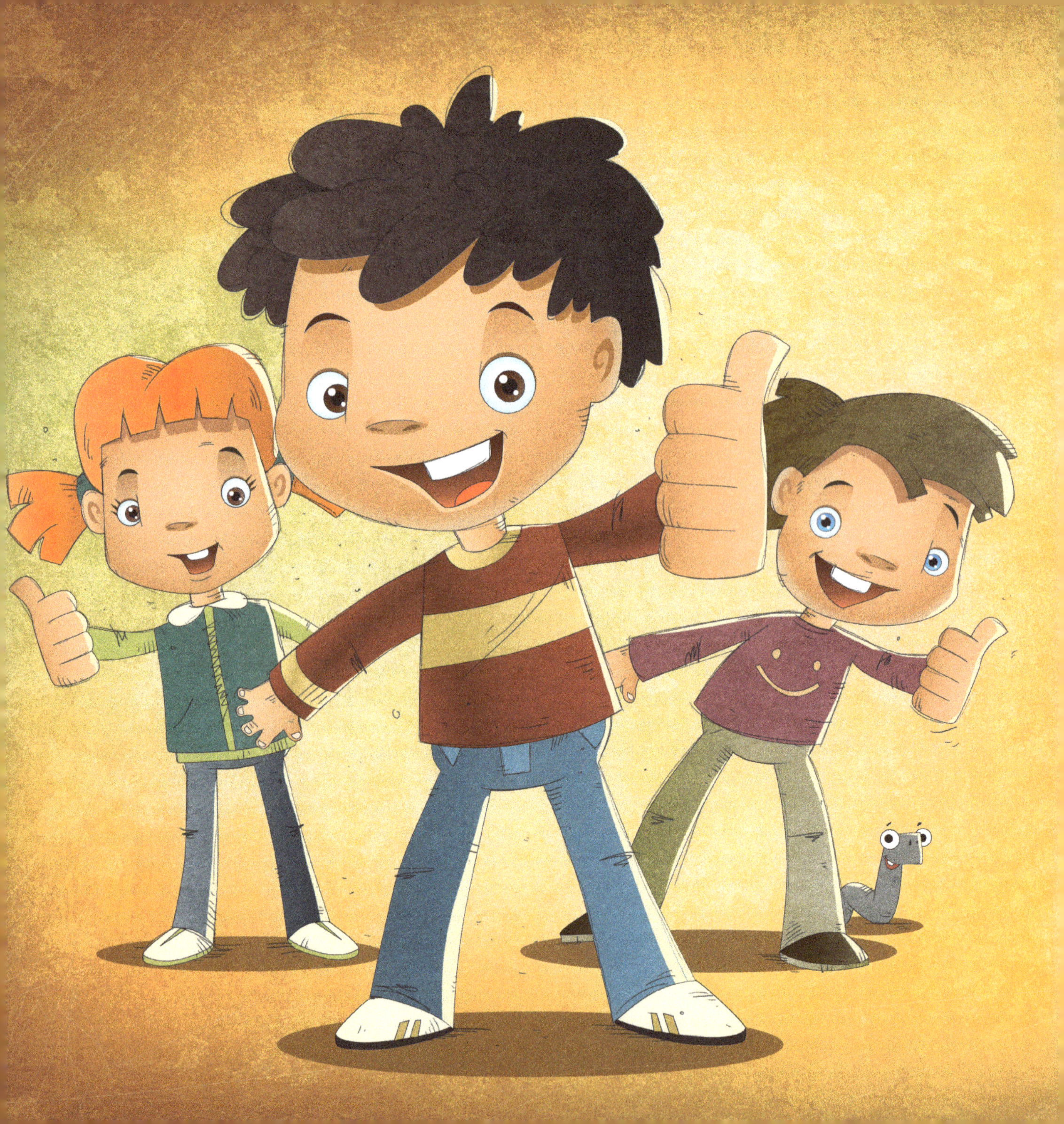

The things you can't change
are perfect as they are...
And if you strive to become better,
you can go pretty far.

Carve your own path
and you'll find your thoughts moved...
To where you are confident
and say, **"I'm self-approved!"**

You're designed to look
exactly the way you do.
Your physical form's
just the outside of you.

**Inside you're much stronger
than you probably know...
Look past your own looks
then you'll truly grow!**

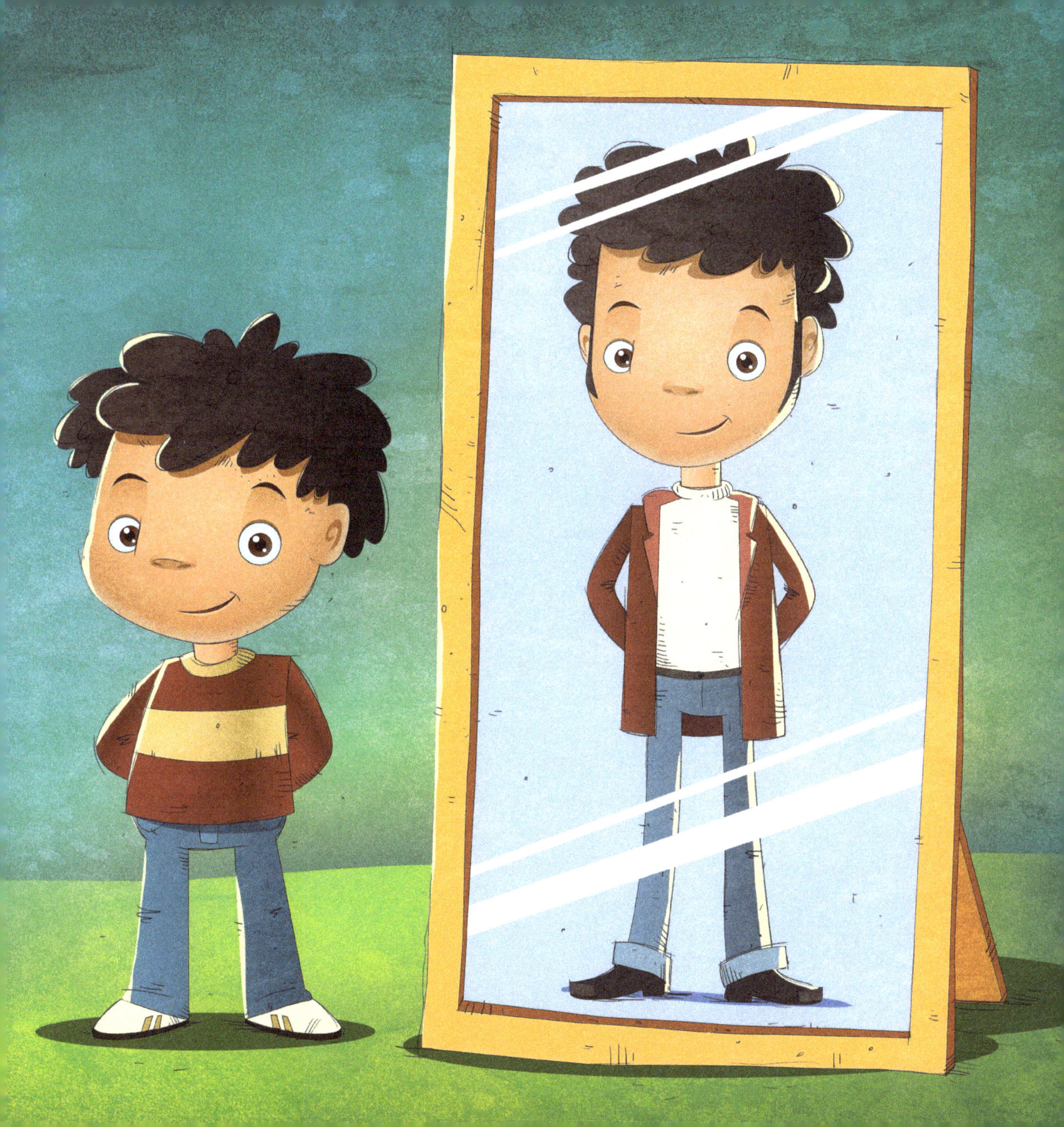

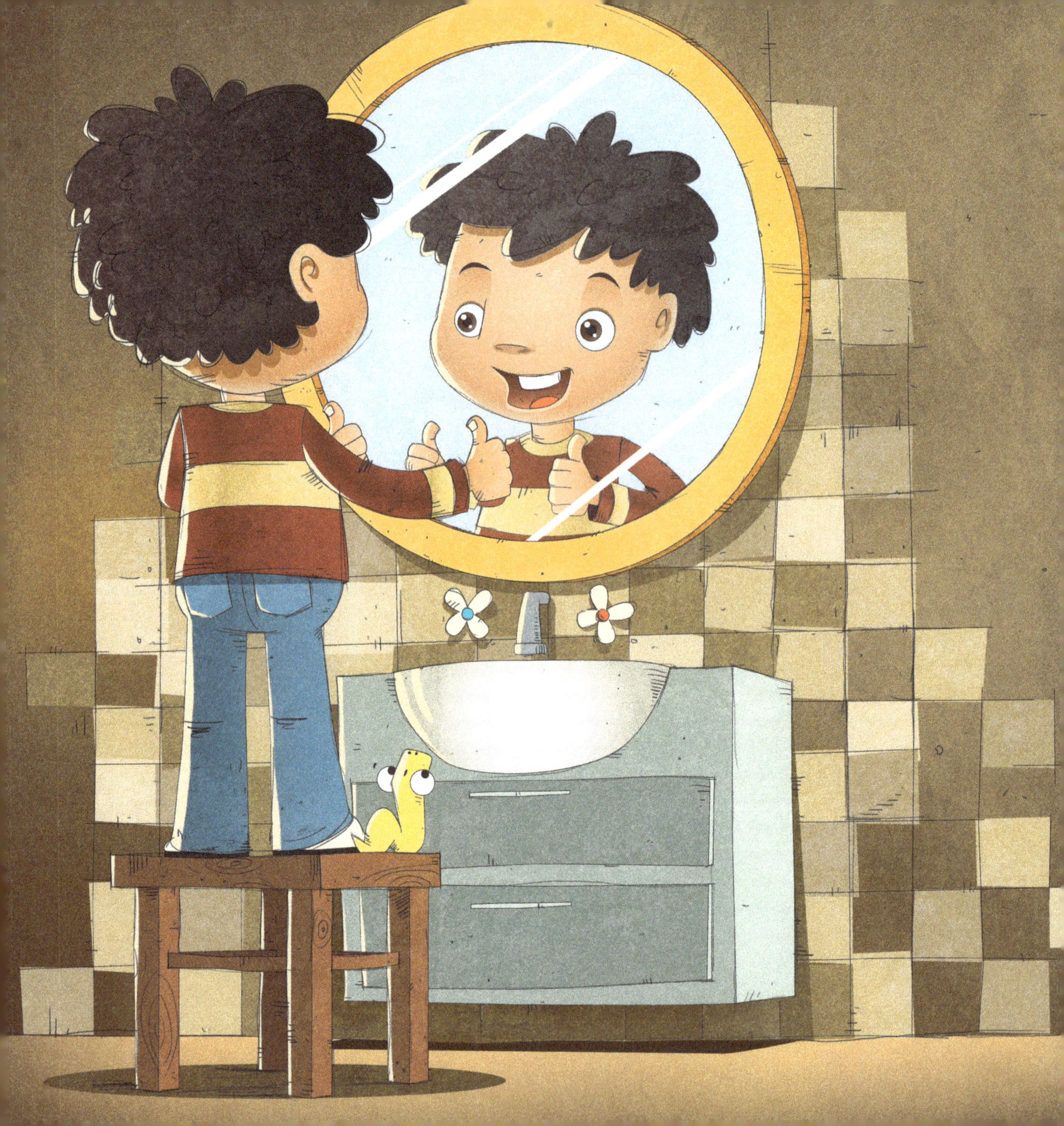

Claim Your FREE Gift!

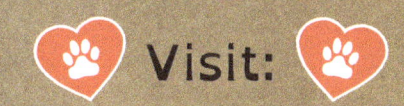

Visit:

PDICBooks.com/Gift

Thank you for purchasing

Stand Up Proud

and welcome to the Puppy Dogs & Ice Cream family. We're certain you're going to love the little gift we've prepared for you at the website above.

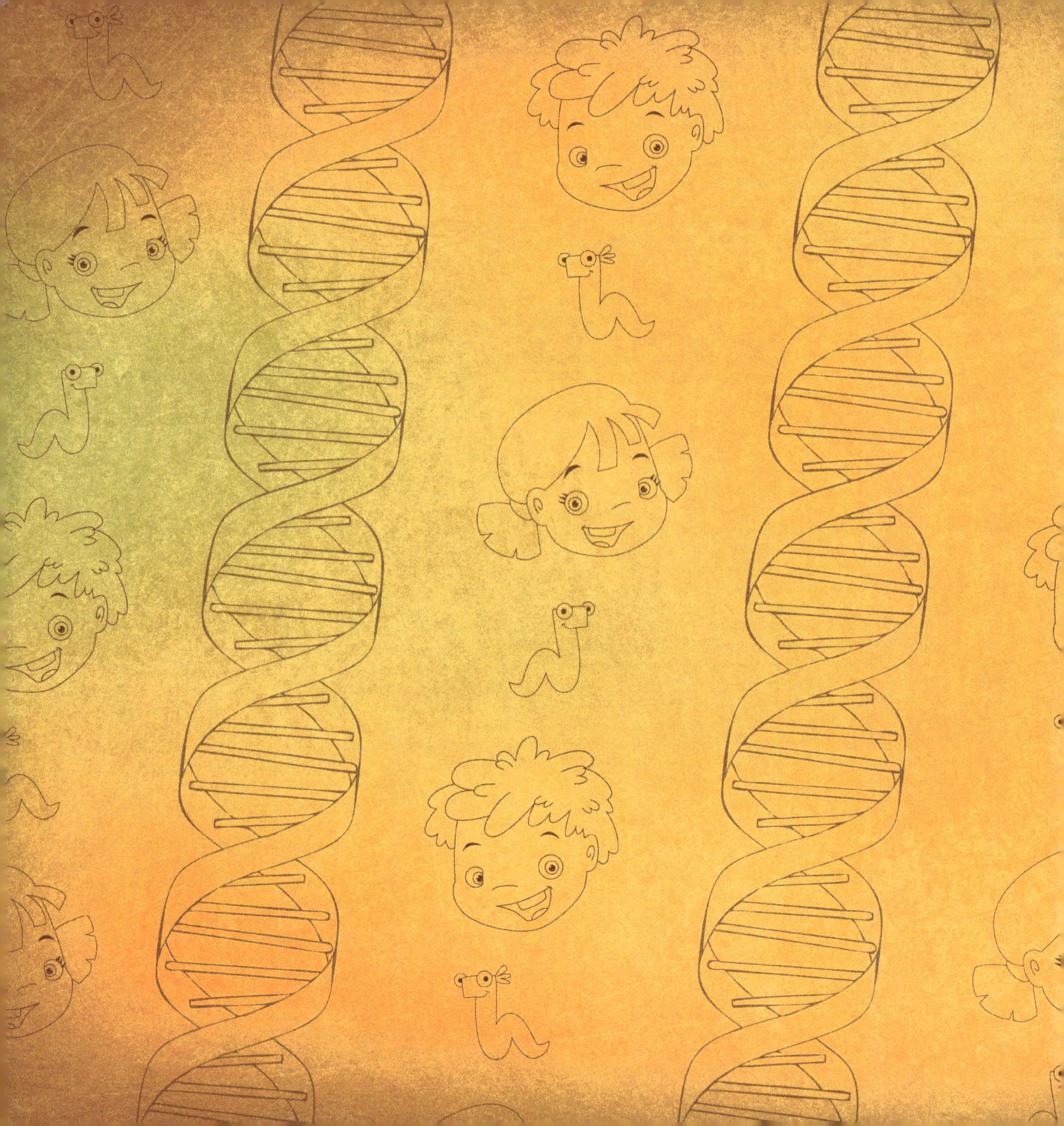

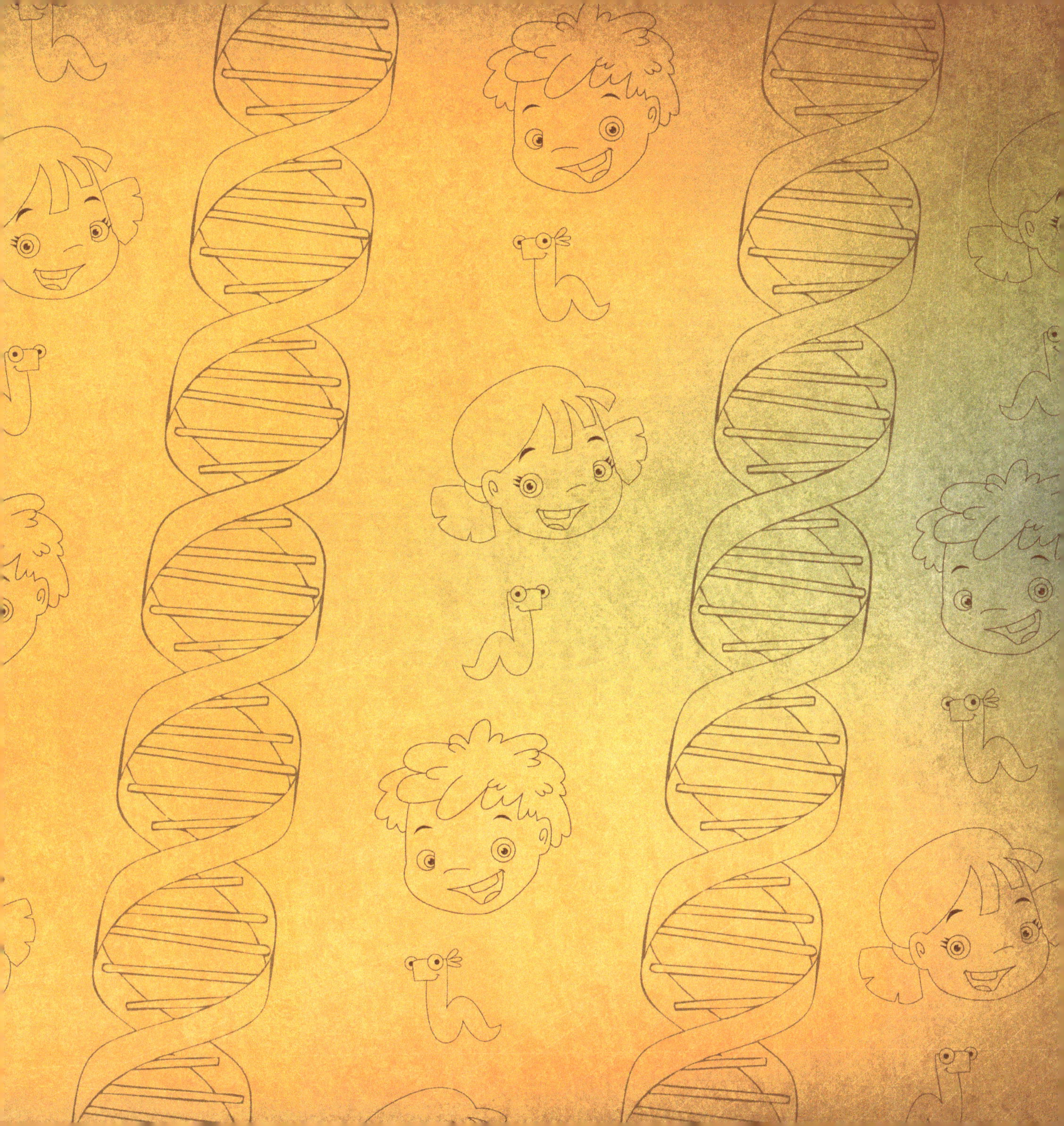